Grandma's Helper

by Lois Meyer
Illustrated by Monique Passicot

ScottForesman
A Division of HarperCollinsPublishers

Grandma met me at the bus stop
with her big shopping bag.
"Mi 'jita, vamos de compras."

"Okay, Grandma," I said.
"I speak Spanish, and English, too.
I can help you shop."

3

In Mrs. Reese's bakery
Grandma said quietly,
"Pan, por favor."
"Bread, please," I said.

5

Grandma put the bread in her big shopping bag.

"Gracias, mi 'jita," she whispered.
Grandma's smile said,
"You're my helper."

In the little store on the corner
Grandma said quietly,
"Leche, por favor."
"Milk, please," I said.

Grandma put the milk in her
big shopping bag.

"Gracias, mi 'jita," she whispered.
Grandma's smile said,
"You're my helper."

At the post office Grandma said quietly, "Estampillas, por favor." "Stamps, please," I said.

Grandma put the stamps in her
big shopping bag.

"Gracias, mi 'jita," she whispered.
Grandma's smile said,
"You're my helper."

At Mr. Salcedo's market
Grandma said, smiling,
"Naranjas, por favor."
"Oranges, please," I said.

MARKET

69 ¢

3 FOR $1⁰⁰

12 ¢ each

99¢

Mr. Salcedo speaks Spanish, and English, too, but Grandma still likes me to help.

Grandma put the oranges in her
big shopping bag.

"Gracias, mi 'jita," she said proudly.
Grandma's smile said,
"You're my helper."

21

At the drug store near my house
Grandma said quietly,
"Un helado, por favor."
"An ice cream, please," I said.

Grandma handed the ice cream to me. It tasted cold and so good.

"Gracias, Grandma," I whispered.
Grandma's smile said, "I love you,
little helper."